Hugh Miller Thompson

First Principles

nine essays from the American Churchman

Hugh Miller Thompson

First Principles
nine essays from the American Churchman

ISBN/EAN: 9783337368463

Printed in Europe, USA, Canada, Australia, Japan

Cover: Foto ©Andreas Hilbeck / pixelio.de

More available books at **www.hansebooks.com**

FIRST PRINCIPLES.

NINE ESSAYS

From the American Churchman,

BY

HUGH MILLER THOMPSON,

Professor of CHURCH HISTORY, in Nashotah Theological Seminary.

Ye have need that one teach you again, which be the FIRST PRINCIPLES of the Oracles of God.—Heb. v. 12.

MILWAUKEE:
H. R. HAYDEN.
New York: POTT & AMERY, Cooper Union.
1869.

TO THE REV. DR. WILLIAM ADAMS,

OF NASHOTAH,

To whom, more than to any man living, I owe whatever of clearness about Christian Doctrine and Duty I profess or teach, I dedicate these Essays.

APOLOGETIC.

IN all our congregations there are a mass of "non-professors," particularly among the men. They are not *dis*-believers, usually. They are not even *un*-believers. The traditions of a Christian Home and training cling to them. They are far from being ready to deny the lessons, or the influences, of their boyhood. But they stand outside all Christian organizations. They will give for the support of Religion, and often, liberally. They will attend Church, often quite regularly, and are always anxious their families should do so. They recognize the value of the Church and the ordinances of religion as guardians of public morality. They will be the personal friends and helpers of the Clergyman—often his warm and generous friends. They are, in hundreds of cases, honorable, upright, large-hearted men, leading their lives, as a matter of fact, on Christian principles of justice and charity. They have every thing but the one thing. They will not "follow ME." They are so much in advance of the young man in the Gospel that they will do the first half of the command. They would, for any really grand and good cause, "sell all they have," and give to the cause; but they do not "Come and follow Me."

It is one of the startling things in our modern religious condition, this that we speak of. It took the writer's mind and thought, from his entrance on his work among these men, as a young and inexperienced Deacon. It has been the phenomenon which has faced him since in every line of Christian effort.

It came to him early that this state of things is largely due to the fact that the modern pulpit *does not speak the language of actual life.* There is a theological dialect— the technical language of a science. It was once taught children, in the days when catechetical instruction was considered a part of pastoral duty. Those days are gone now, alas! from among most Christian denominations. The pulpit, however, still retains the obsolete dialect, and that dialect positively brings no meaning to the ears of the busy layman. The preacher is setting forth the language and the phrases of the theological "system," whatever it may be, in which he was trained, and which he preaches; and the words go by the pre-occupied hearer, engaged in the practical work of life, as empty sounds.

Perhaps there has been less of this mistake in the writer's own Communion. There, also, the catechetical instruction of the young is an active ministerial duty still, and those brought up within the body come to listen to the instructions of the pulpit acquainted with whatever slight technicality of phrase is used in the simple teachings of a body which especially clings to Scripture terms.

But the mass of hearers in that body are from without, and the body itself is not, relatively, large. It is influenced by the general tone. So, everywhere, it seemed to him, that the pulpit too often talked of the past, to the men of the past, in the language of the past. It failed to come, in plain, homely, un-technical speech, home to the very wants and struggles of the busy men who sat before it—men whose problems and puzzles and temptations, are those of this day and this hour.

This seemed one cause of the enormous non-professorship. Another cause, and the original—the writer found in the sadly wrecked and torn state of a divided Christianity, in the jealousy, bitterness and Godlessness of a sectarianism that is the curse of American Christianity.

With the last cause he could not deal, except, in his own small way, to preach and practice the catholic truth and faith, in love and charity. With regard to the other, it should be the aim of the clergy so to speak to men— so to present the Gospel without subtlety, in plain, homely English—that the men of our own time should feel it to be a thing for them—that they should recognize in it the answers to American questions as well as Jewish, to nineteenth century troubles as well as first century troubles. They should try to strip from it every tradition of human interpretation, and present it direct, in the direct words which their neighbors use.

The following essays were written for that large class who have been mentioned—not for infidels, or godless, or scoffers—but for Christian men who will not assume the Christian name; for the hundreds of warm friends the writer has, and the thousands like those friends, who do not come forward like men and shoulder the duty of their lives. The writer has only tried to bring out the thought, strongly, clearly and kindly.

While the essays were in course of publication, he had good reason to know that they had been found a help, by many, on the road to light. They were copied, some of them, into a number of the secular and religious papers of different names.

The writer took it as a sign that they were found telling for their purpose, and readable.

Meanwhile a number of Bishops, Clergy, and Laymen, suggested their re-publication, in their present shape. That suggestion is justification enough for re-publishing hasty newspaper articles, and for hoping they may be thus found more largely useful, by laity and clergy alike.

They were written from the writer's heart. May GOD's blessing go with them to the hearts of others.

NASHOTAH, Feast of St. Luke, 1869.

First Principles.

CHAPTER I.

Responsibility.

THE great responsibilities of life, no man chooses. They are imposed without his consent asked.

Existence itself, which includes all the rest, the awful responsibility of *living*, no man accepts or refuses. He is not called into council. The responsibility, and all its endless issues, are laid upon him, whether he will or no.

The place, too, in which he shall live, and the circumstances under which he shall grow up, and by which he shall be trained, are all determined for him beforehand.

He finds himself *born* a citizen (let us say) of the United States. He was not consulted about the matter. This citizenship, and all its duties, all its privileges and all its obligations, are laid on his shoulders, whether he will or no.

He finds himself born into civilization. There are responsibilities growing out of that. He must face them, willingly or unwillingly.

So one may run through the whole roll. The duties

and obligations of life, and of a special form of life; of
life in a particular land, and under particular laws and
special circumstances, are all *imposed*. A man does not
choose them. He finds them upon him. And conscience
and the common judgment of mankind, and the law of
nature, as well as the law of God, demand that he shall
bear them, and answer for the manner of that bearing.

A sensible man, an honest man, faces the facts. Here
is his life, and here are its various responsibilities—*here*,
and not yonder. He has to live the life of a freeman,
and not of a slave; the life of a civilized man, not that
of a savage; the life of an educated man, and not the
life of a South Sea Islander. He has to live the life of a
citizen, a member of a civilized community, owing duties
in a hundred directions to others. He has to live as son
and brother, as husband and father. He may, at times,
stagger under the burden of duty so laid upon him un-
sought. Men have sometimes honestly wished they had
never been educated! Men have, more than once, expressed regret that they were not born in some half bar-
barous land! For a man may well shrink from the responsibilities of even enlightenment and civilization.

But there is no chance for shrinking. To these things
a man is *elected*, by the good pleasure of his Supreme
Master; and he must face them and answer for them.

And as we say, the sensible man does face them. He
accepts the situation, and rises to its duties. He is per-
fectly sure there can be, in the nature of things, no shirking. A man is judged *by what he has*. God determines
the measure of his duty, beforehand.

Now, as it is in all else in life, so also it is in religion.
There is, for those who will read this writing, no choice
allowed. In a vague way, we speak of the duty of men

to be Christians. We urge them to "become Christians." From the pulpit, we hear men persuaded to accept Christianity. In a vague way, all this is right enough.

But when we examine, we find that there is really a fallacy here, unless we carefully distinguish.

There is no choice in the case. A man is born into the responsibilities of Christianity, as he is born into those of citizenship. He cannot refuse the former, any more than the latter. For him, the question of Christianity has been determined, long since.

The first words that struck his perceptions were *Christian* words. Perhaps the earliest was a Christian prayer. Christian words and ideas were round him like an atmosphere, in the cradle. He was lulled to sleep with Christian songs. The standard of right and wrong brought to his opening intelligence, was a Christian standard. He grew up surrounded by the results of Christianity on all sides. The books he read were saturated with Christian sentiment. The studies he pursued were taught him because he was to be a Christian man. The law of the land, and the subtler law of social ethics and good manners, which hemmed him in, and under which he grew, are what they are because of Christianity.

And now, after all this training, (all the moral ideas he possesses, all the spiritual development he has reached being Christian,) he stands surrounded still with Christianity, visible and alive. Turn where he will, Church doors stand open for him, Bibles are at his hand, Fonts await him, and the Minister stands ready. Altars display the memorials of the eternal Sacrifice. Pulpits announce the Gospel, and cry in warning; and all things are ready.

Clearly these things are all facts of a man's position.

Neglect of them does not annihilate them. Disbelief in them does not change them. They are parts of the sum of life to the man living under them. He can do nothing with them but face them and answer for them, as he does for all the rest.

Neglect of his duty as a citizen, denial of his duty as a member of community or of the family, does not change or remove the relations, or any responsibility of the relations. A man may make his whole life empty, fruitless, vile, by fighting at cross purposes with these facts of existence, if he will. But no man ever dreams that their burden does not lie upon him; and all men judge him, and judge him rightly, by the measure of these facts. If he make a wreck of his life, it is a civilized man's , a free man's, an educated man's, an intelligent man's life that is wrecked. This was what was given; and for this inquiry shall be made at last. *It was also a Christian life that has gone to ruin!*

It is not then a thing to be determined to-day by any man who reads this, whether he will be a Christian. That was determined for him by the free election of his God. He was *born under* the law of Christianity, as he was under the law of civilization. Christianity is one of the facts of life which he cannot shirk; one of the responsibilities that must be answered for.   .

Whatever law is Christian, that law rests on each man's soul here. Whatever hope is Christian, is freely given to each. Whatever light Christianity reveals, is a free light to all. Whatever morality, whatever sum of human duty Christianity announces, that is the morality and that the duty demanded of every soul, in this land, at least.

These are things beyond us. We cannot alter them.

A man may fret and complain; but that does not change
the fact. He is under Christianity. He is judged by
Christianity. His neighbors measure his life by the
Christian law. GOD will measure it by the same. And
he is his own witness that GOD and man do righteously,
for he measures himself by it. His conscience, as far as
it gives a clear utterance at all, is a Christian conscience,
educated under Christian influences!

When men are urged, from pulpit, or by writing, to
" become Christians," the real meaning is that they are
urged to become *good* Christians. They are not to dream
that Christianity is a voluntary matter, which they can
accept or reject at will, and be blameless.

The point of the preacher's persuasion is, not to get a
man to adopt a responsibility which is not his till he does
adopt it. It is to get him to rise to a responsibility
which is his in any case. He seeks to persuade a man
to meet his life, as that life is given. He urges him to
accept things as they are; and, since he *is* tried, and
will be forever tried by Christian law, warns him to take
that law as the measure of his life, just as GOD gave it.

It is one of the prevailing delusions, (and one, we fear,
which the common pulpit seldom reaches,) to suppose
that a man is free to accept or refuse the responsibilities
of the Christian life—that "the professing of Christianity" is the taking up of new and quite voluntary duties.

We distinctly write it down a delusion; and such a
shallow delusion, that it will stand no test. It is a flat
contradiction of human life, and of the facts of human
life, that stare us all in the face.

The profession of CHRIST is not the taking up of a
single duty which is not binding on every man, at least
in lands like this, already. The baptized man has bound

himself to nothing which is not on the unbaptized man as well. The communicant is measured by no rule which is not used righteously also for the non-communicant. There are not two classes of people in a Christian country, under two different laws—the "professors" under one, and the "non-professors" under another.

By God's divine ordering of human life, we are *elected* to Christianity. *Why*, we cannot tell. It is His "good pleasure." *It is the fact*—that is all we know about it and all, that, as sensible people, we should care to know. Our plain business is to "make the election *sure*."

To profess Christ, then, is merely to shoulder, willingly, a man's bounden duty. A man makes up his mind not to fight against his position, not to make a wreck of his life by living at cross purposes with it. He concludes to take God's design as wisest and best for him. He determines to accept God's purposes, and rise to their meaning, and bring himself into harmony with the facts of his position.

We put this matter here designedly in this common-sense and practical view, for common sense and practical people. We put it so, because it has been so sadly confused in the minds of so many. Men need to look at things as they are, and measure life by its plain, visible, measures. They need to be warned not to cheat themselves in religion, as they would not dare to do in any common matter.

And, plainly and practically, every man who reads this is under every duty and every responsibility of Christianity, as he is under every duty and every responsibility of citizenship in the land.

His wise way, his only manly and honest way, is to stand up boldly, trusting in the God who put him where he is, and accept the work and duty laid out before his face.

Men in thousands are living poor, fragmentary, fruitless, failing lives—because, like cowards, they are shirking the bounden duty of their place, and shutting their eyes to things as unalterable as the courses of the stars.

It is not, then for you, reader, unbaptized or non-communicant, to decide whether you will be a Christian or not. This only is left you to decide, whether you will be a Christian in truth and reality, or whether you will fight the purpose of God in putting you here, and spend your life in fruitless efforts to be as near a heathen as you can. Fruitless efforts—make sure of that, for your place is fixed, and, by the law of Christ, here and everywhere, and by that only, can *you* be measured, and *your* life be tried!

CHAPTER II.

Salvation.

THE preaching of the Gospel is a proclamation of *salvation*. From the first the announcement to men has been—how they might be saved.

What is this salvation a salvation *from?* When a man asks to be saved, what is he to be saved *from?* From *what* is a man's soul to be delivered by his Saviour?

We fear the common answer is, *from punishment.* We even fear that the pulpit, very often, conveys that answer, unconsciously to itself, to the ordinary hearer.

Salvation means—to most, we think—*salvation from penalty.* When they are saved, they are saved from pain. Christ came to deliver, in the common mind, from the punishment due to sin. And since the many consider salvation to be only a deliverance from punishment—and, since this world (they are taught) is not a world of retribution, but a world of probation—and, since only in the other world real penalty and real reward come—it therefore results, that salvation, being a deliverance from punishment, is a thing which belongs solely to another existence. It comes, after a man has died. It consists in his not going to hell.

With this as the view of salvation, it is impossible not to be confused, on the very first principles of Christianity. Faith, repentance, duty, hope, all are referred to another life. Religion is valuable, as providing for one's well being *there*. The Gospel is postponed, as to all its highest benefits and blessings, to another existence. Salvation is future, and not present. The warnings and exhortations of Revelation are misinterpreted by this false first idea. A man mistakes his real danger—and runs into it while seeking to avoid an imaginary danger.

Salvation *is* deliverance from punishment; but as a secondary result. First of all, it is deliverance from sin. Salvation from penalty follows as a result of being saved from transgression. The SAVIOUR has this name, because He comes to " save His people from their *sins*." The Gospel is a proclamation of deliverance from a present curse. It has reference to this life and this world. It is the preaching of some blessing, which is to be possessed *here* and *now*. And that is salvation and deliverance, in body, soul, and spirit, from iniquity, from transgression, from rebellion against GOD.

It is not punishment that ruins a man; but the sin that entails the punishment. It is not pain that destroys; but the transgression which brings the pain. It is not misery from which a man need cry to be delivered; but, from the rebellion against GOD which has brought that misery.

Salvation, then, is salvation from sin—deliverance out of it—victory over it—mastery and conquest of the enemy inside a man, which is eating his life out.

It belongs to this life and this world. It is to be prayed for, sought for, worked for, and fought for, *here*. In this world, a man may be saved, nay *must* be, if he is ever to be saved anywhere. He is in a state of salvation, a saved and delivered state, in this visible world; or he has no assurance of such a state in any world.

First of all, we need to be clear on this. Error, here, will produce error in all our thoughts of practical religion.

Where the main aim and end of Christianity is taken to be simply deliverance from penalty—where it is valued solely as offering the means of escape from penal suffering—we have postponed repentance, deferred amendment, blundering death-bed preparations. And then we have again, that wonderful and sickening sight, of men—who see no value in the life and death of the LORD, to men, except to assure them against the consequences of their sins—turning round, and declaring there are no such consequences; and, as there is no damnation, there is consequently no salvation!

The shallowness of Universalism has had its success, solely, because men have supposed salvation to be deliverance from punishment; and from a particular kind of punishment, too—punishment after death. It has been received, because the popular pulpit has preached a salvation which is not that of the Gospel—a salvation *in* sin, and a salvation *from* punishment. The matter is just reversed. GOD proclaims salvation in terms precisely contradictory. *His* salvation is *from* sin, while, as in David's case, it may be *in* punishment. A man may be —nay, often *is*—saved *in* punishment, and even *by* punishment. He can never be saved in sin, much less can he be saved *by* sin.

We press this. It is the shallowness of modern preaching—this Gospel of escape from pain. It is the shallowness and deadness of modern religion—this selfish Gospel of deliverance from suffering. It has divorced religion from every-day duty, and from common life. It has turned her out of the counting-house, and the market, and the shop. It has made her a mere insurance against some vague future suffering. It has represented her to men as a plan of escape from future flame. It has allowed them to go all their lives, lost and ruined, living in a present damnation, and yet hoping for a salvation that is to come.

Pain! surely, in the light of Christianity, no man can hold *pain* accursed. The "Man of Sorrows" led a life of pain. His religion is the very sanctification of pain. Its very centre, as a practical thing, is the blessedness of pain—that sorrow and agony, borne, that others may not bear them—that misery and anguish, drunk to the dregs, that others may be spared them—is the road, forevermore, to peace and blessedness!

With Gethsemane and Calvary before a man, it is hard to see how a Christian can imagine that the whole purpose of his life is to shun suffering; and that the eternal purpose and value of his Faith are, that, by it he escapes pain!

We must go back to the first principles, here, more clearly than we have yet done. The old Gospel of salvation *from sin* must be preached with more care and more pronounced distinctness, because of this terrible confusion of the popular pulpit.

To deliver men from the slavery of sin—to deliver them by pain, and through pain—came hither the HOLY ONE. To make possible, and to proclaim, the salvation of a man from the rot that rots his heart out, from the bitter ruin that overwhelms his soul, from the sin that poisons him by inches, body, soul, and spirit—to do this our LORD came. He knew the enemy. He knew the curse. He did not mistake causes for effects. He came to "save His people from their *sins*." That salvation was through untold agony to Him; and must be, to the end, through bitter anguish to them. He proclaimed no reversal of the moral laws of the Universe. He did not make it possible that a man be lost in sin, and yet saved from the penalty of sin. He divorced not ruin from ruin's causes. They are forever bound together, by the laws of God's unchangeable nature.

We therefore preach *salvation from sin*. We tell men that the Lord came hither, and took our nature, and lived and died, and rose, to make it possible for a man to be delivered from this curse and ruin which is bound up in his nature.

That curse and ruin every man knows is there. Its existence is no part of the *peculiar* revelation of Christianity. Persius, the heathen poet, recognized its existence, as readily as St. Paul. Christianity only finds it there; takes it as it is, teaches its nature, and makes salvation from it possible.

The man that accepts this salvation, enters on a course of warfare with this curse. He undertakes a life-long struggle with it. He knows it will ruin him utterly, to the last fiber of his nature, if he do not get rid of it. Therefore he accepts the preached salvation, and in Christ's Name and way, stands up like a man, and faces his enemy. He is sure to meet trouble, sure to encounter pain, sure to suffer anguish. A suffering Christ has sanctified all these to salvation's uses. But in these—neck deep in these—he is a *saved man*. Already he is delivered from the power of sin; and, every day, he is becoming more and more delivered, through the faith, and by the power, of the Lord.

At the start. then, when a man accepts the offers of
salvation, and desires to embrace them and be saved, let
him be distinctly taught that it is a *present* world's work
and business on which he is entering. It involves deliverance from hell, necessarily, of course; but, because it
takes for granted, deliverance from sin.

It is something, also, which he has to win himself, by
downright work. It is God's free gift in Christ; that
is true; but like all God's free gifts—the sunlight, and
the summer rain, and the fruitful field—can only be
made an individual blessing, a personal possession, by a
man's own effort. Therefore, salvation for any single
soul is to be wrought out by that soul's own toil and
tears. On the anvil of holy resolution, a man beats out
into shape the work of his life. And the sweat rains on
the hot iron, and the breath comes sobbing, and the
muscles strain, and he longs for the evening hour of
rest; but he, and he only, can do this which the Great
Master has given, this special work—the working out of
his own salvation with trembling and fear.

The proclamation of salvation, the good news of God
—this is it: That a man *now*, by Christ's Birth and Life
and Passion, by His Resurrection, Ascension, and the
gift of His Holy Spirit in His own Church and Kingdom,
can be saved from the slavery of sin, and can work out
his own deliverance more fully, every hour he lives.

And first, to understand the rest—Salvation means
work—hard work, and present work—work in *this* world.
It belongs to us here. A man's evidence that he will be
saved when he is dead, is that he is now saved while he
is alive.

CHAPTER III.

FAITH.

THE Apostles of the LORD, after His Ascension, went forth and preached the good news of salvation and deliverance, over all the world. To make that good news of any value, it was first necessary that it should be *believed*. Faith, therefore, was the very first requirement for salvation. Faith is so always.

And here metaphysical systems of theology have come in to bewilder plain people. Seeing how high a place Faith occupies in the New Testament—how we are said to be *saved* through Faith, and justified by Faith—these systems have drawn distinctions and divided hairs in definitions; have tried to analyze and dissect Faith; have tried to tell us just what "justifying" Faith is, and what it is not; so that, in one such system, we have seventeen kinds of Faith defined, none of which is that particular kind called saving, or justifying.

It would really seem that the Gospel was meant to save some few of us who may not be metaphysicians. It would be only reasonable, one would think, to hope that a man can be a Christian without being a master in logical science.

Let us see if we cannot understand, without much logic, the place which Faith occupies in this matter of salvation.

Remember, then, what salvation is—deliverance from the power of sin, from its guilt, its stain, its ruin, its destruction. The Gospel is the Good News that tells a man *how* that deliverance may be obtained. It proclaims that CHRIST has died and obtained a free pardon for all sinners, which pardon is offered to all that will take it. It declares, too, that He has organized, in this world, an army, a host, of those who are pardoned, who are banded together to fight against sin while life lasts, as the one thing detestable and accursed. It declares to him that CHRIST revealed, here on earth, in His words and works, His life and death, the law of Heaven, and organized that law in His own Kingdom—a society formed here, and visible to all men's eyes, the Church and Kingdom of GOD, where that law is supreme, and where men accept it, as the rule of life and salvation. It tells him that the man who would be saved, must accept the offered pardon or amnesty for the past; must swear off from sin, as the one ruin and curse and rottenness of human nature ; must forswear the world, with its temporary cheats and delusions, the devil and his service, the flesh and its slavery ; must recognize the plain truth that wrong, and lies, and vileness, are the deadly enemies, the ruin and destruction, of man made in GOD's image, and that human salvation is in conquering and trampling on these. It tells him that his business is to place himself at once in deadly hostility, in sworn enmity, to these, for time and for eternity.

Here, plainly, are things announced which demand, from every man, personal action. If the story of CHRIST's life and death be true, it gives a new coloring to all life and all effort. It lays downright work on a man. There is a course of duty before him, a plain road laid out for him to travel.

He could not have found it for himself. On the whole the world, visible and tangible, does *not* tell him that sin is his ruin. Looking at that, it seems as if wrong and lies were very often the road to success and deliverance. The visible world puts cheats upon him. He sees the bad man prosper, the good man in great tribulation. He sees successful fraud, prosperous injustice, profitable wrong. For this day and the next, for this year and the next, the bad thing seems to conquer the good thing, the lie seems better than the truth. His senses and his worldly knowledge appear to tell him that salvation, prosperity, happiness and success, may be, in this world, and for this time, at least, won by evil and falsehood. The devil does seem to be master and king *here*, however it may be in other worlds and other ages.

And here comes this Gospel, announcing the direct reverse of all his senses tell him. It comes, declaring that all these appearances of successful and profitable evil are only cheating phantoms of a passing day, only the exceptional and disappearing shadows of an hour. It declares that, let the world appear as it will, sin cannot be successful, wrong cannot be profitable, lies cannot be good. It proclaims that GOD is King here, too; that sin is accursed in this world, as it is in all worlds. It contradicts the fleeting appearances of time, and proclaims, on earth, the everlasting laws of GOD's eternal Kingdom—that sin is ruin, that wrong is forever death, that lies are evermore destruction to all GOD's creatures. It cries over all the world, that in this rebel realm, as in the very white heavens of GOD, the sole salvation and peace for any child of the King is, that he put himself in conscious and avowed hostility—in sworn enmity and deadly hatred—to every sin, to every wrong, to every lie, as against GOD's nature, and therefore against his own. It tells him that the very SON of GOD, Himself, came here on earth, to proclaim, in the midst of all its delusions, the law of Heaven, as the one unchanging and everlasting law of life for every responsible creature of His Father.

And here is Faith. The man that believes this announcement has Faith. He accepts it as something from above the world. It arises, not from human experience, but from divine revelation. It appeals, not to his sight, but to his insight; not to his experience, but to his spirit, his higher reason. It is a truth from a sphere beyond. It comes to him as belonging to eternity, and not to time; as belonging to Heaven, and not to earth. If he accept it, he must accept it by Faith and not by sight.

Its acceptance runs to the roots of life. That is clear. It reverses his whole view of the world, and of his own business in the world. It changes the color of the entire universe. It puts another face on all his days. It lets down here about him the white light of heaven, and tells him to walk by that, and not by the falsehoods of sense. If he see fraud profitable, it declares he shall believe it unprofitable, notwithstanding. If he see wrong triumphant, it tells him to deny his eyes, and hold to the last that wrong is ruinous. If he see sin pleasant, and the source of happiness, it insists that he shall contradict his eyes and senses, and hold sin bitter and vile, and the one source of endless misery and woe, now and always.

This world, it tells him, is an exceptional world, the one rebel realm in all GOD's vast Universe. He must understand it so. He must therefore walk by the law, and not by the exception. He must live here, not on the principles of the realm that has rebelled, but on those of the grand whole which has not rebelled, where God's eternal law of right, and truth, and love, rules in power.

If he accept this story, he has Faith, we say. He can accept it only by Faith. Observation and knowledge would never have taught it. The rebels around him never could have told him. It is brought to him from above, and he must believe it on trust.

Now if he accept it to act on it, it is *saving* Faith. If his reception of the announcement be so strong and so hearty that he, seeing salvation is an entirely practical matter, prepares to act on these facts and principles, and sets about working, doing, and living, then he has a Faith which saves him.

For his salvation consists in working, doing and living; not merely in professing, feeling and talking. He is, as we have seen, to conquer sin inside himself; to fight it, all his life, outside. He is to cleanse his heart, and cleanse his hands, from stain. He is to live by the law of Heaven. He is to reduce himself to obedience under that law. He is saved when he does it. He is lost when he does it not. If he practice fraud, he ruins himself. If he do injustice to the meanest of God's creatures, he curses himself. If he give way to lust, he damns himself. If he trust in lies, he links himself to hell. If he live on robbery or wrong, he makes a covenant with death. These things are his destruction. He did not know this till Christ came, and lived and died to tell him.

He believes that life and death, and sets to work to conquer death, and work out his own deliverance. He then has *saving* Faith.

And this Faith, like salvation, is a present, active thing. It belongs here, to this world, and is for this world's work.

Unfortunately, there is another kind of Faith, quite too common. There is a faith very good for eternity, but very useless for time; a Faith very strong for some other world, and very weak for this poor dark one, where it is especially needed.

We have seen men who can trust God for Heaven, but cannot trust Him for the earth; who believe in Him for after death, but have no confidence in Him for life? Here they must depend on their own smartness—on their own tact, shrewdness, and sharp dealing. They have Faith, on Sundays, for eternity, in God. On Mondays, when they come to drive bargains—to buy, sell, and get gain—they have confidence only in their own acuteness and the maxims of the godless world!

A real saving Faith is a thing to live on. A man must take it into his shop, his office, his counting-room, into the market, and on 'Change. He must buy and sell on it. He must live with it, at home and on the street. He must have it over his ledger, as well as over his Prayer Book. He can tell whether it is *saving* by that plain test.

For, as we have seen, it is the hearty reception of principles and facts, which give an utterly new meaning to *this* life and to *this* world. It is the acceptance of a law which contradicts the law of sense and time.

The man who accepts those facts and principles, and adopts this law, in sincerity, walks and lives and acts by unseen realities, by eternal and changeless rules, which were supreme before the earth sprang from chaos, and which shall still be supreme, after

"The wreck of matter and the crash of worlds."

He is saved now, and saved forever, because he stands under the everlasting law of God, revealed on earth by the LORD CHRIST, the law of Sonship towards GOD, and therefore of armed hatred to sin.

CHAPTER IV.

REPENTANCE.

IF we have understood SALVATION rightly, it will be easier to understand Repentance and its connection with Salvation.

When the Apostles went forth to proclaim deliverance to all the world, and men asked them "What shall we *do* to be saved?" the answer is first—"Repent ye!"

For already, evidently, they *believed.* They could not otherwise, have asked the question. They must have accepted the story—have believed the preaching—or they could not have reached the point of saying, "Men and brethren, what shall we *do?*"

"Repent ye!" comes next—"Change your minds; alter your purposes; turn right about; reverse your aims, your motives, and your lives." This is the real meaning of the full and comprehensive Greek expression translated "REPENT!"

When a man repents, it does not mean merely that he is sorry for a mistake; that he regrets an error; that he is annoyed and chagrined at his own loss of self-respect from a moral fall.

All these may exist, and the man's feelings may be very much agitated, very intense, and very deep, and yet there may be no *repentance.*

Sorrow, therefore, is not repentance; deep contrition

and anguish of heart are not repentance. A man may seek, as Esau did, "a place of repentance carefully *and with tears*," and may, like him, find none. And no *depth* or *intensity* of sorrow or contrition is repentance. That is, repentance is not merely a more intense degree of sorrow.

Sorrow and anguish of soul may be attendants upon repentance. They may lead to it. But, likewise, they may not. There is no necessary connection.

But to insist on them as essential, to judge of the sincerity of a man's repentance by the intensity of his sorrow, or the abundance of his groanings, is utterly to mistake the Gospel, and to mislead the man.

A man is going on the road of ruin. He is the slave of sin. It is eating the heart out of him. He is asleep, or blind or deaf, in mere slavery to the world, the devil, or his own flesh.

To such a man the Gospel comes. It reveals his ruin, and the road of safety from that ruin. It shows him how utterly blind, stupid and mean his life and purposes are. It points out separation from God as the one bitter curse; sin, as the one evil against which he and all men are to struggle. It tells him how he can struggle successfully now—how he can, by the help secured, have good hope of victory.

He believes the story. He has been a deluded man so far. In the light of the story of the life and death of the Lord, his life is madness, and its end confusion.

So he *repents*. He turns right about; that is, changes his notions, his purposes, his aims. What he loved he now abhors. What he once considered harmless, he now flies, as the pestilence. A new light has broken over human life; a splendor from heaven has baptized the world and the world's walks. He sees things as they are now. He begins to measure things at their real value, to understand them in their real connections. He reads the riddle of life backward no more. He begins at the right end. He turns right about to live in the new light, and by the new knowledge in which he believes, and thus *repents*.

It may come, this reversal of his course, in bitterness of soul, in anguish and sore agony, in grim wrestle with the devil. It may come, with the triumphant joy of self-conquest, with the calm repose of determined self-control. It may come, in blinding grief for a past that has been wrong and false, or in high hope for a future, that by God's grace, shall be right and true.

But come as it will, the repentance is the *turning about*, the reversal of a man's position towards God, the changing of his whole mind about himself, his Maker, and the Universe.

And, clearly this is not a thing done once and ended. Repentance, from the nature of man, is not an *act*, but a *state*. It lasts, like Faith, through life. A man begins his Christian course with repentance, and ends it with repentance. In all Catholic Liturgies, repentance is a perpetual accompaniment of every act of worship, a necessary preparation for every sacrament. The young beginner professes repentance at the very threshhold. The oldest Bishop, gray in the Christian service, professes it with the palms and the crown before his dying eyes. It is the poor shallowness and weakness of popular Christianity, that it has utterly lost the very knowledge of repentance, and its place in the Christian life. St. Augustine repents all his life. Athanasius—spotless and clear, calm, stern, and fearless, like one of God's armed archangels—prays as a penitent all the fifty years that, in the LORD's Holy Name, he fights the world. In our own times and in our own Church, KEN, the saintliest soul in England, dies a penitent, as he had lived. And all the great and holy, all the heroes of Christianity, all the stainless names that flame along the story of the Church Catholic in all lands and times—all lived and died penitents—repentance and faith their companions to the end! It is left for the poor emptiness of modern religionism, to make repentance a half hour's hysterical excitement in a hot meeting-house, under blazing gas lights.

A man is to live all his life in repentance. He is not only to turn about, but to stay turned; not only to change his mind, but to keep it changed.

Repentance, therefore, is a part of that state in which a man lives and holds himself with relation to GOD. Faith is one part. He must believe that GOD is, and that He is a rewarder of such as diligently seek Him. Repentance is another. He must stand as GOD's servant, as GOD's son.

Sin is his ruin professed. Evil is his curse. Lies are his destruction. He faces these things as deadly foes. Once they were friends; once he looked for good from them. Heaven's light has come down upon him and the world. He has opened his eyes and looked at things in that light, and is cheated no more. He now stands, consciously to himself, the sworn enemy of sin. He can make no compromise. He can strike hands with it in no truce. The wrong thing, the false thing, the foul, the bad thing in himself and in the world, is the thing utterly detestable and hateful to him, utterly ruinous to him and all men.

He has turned about, changed his mind, under the brightness of "the Light that lighteneth all men," and holds that relation to these things, and insists that they shall hold it towards him. It is a world-long war between him and these, henceforth.

Towards God the relation is changed also. He now looks toward God as the only fit Master for man. He looks to Him for hope, for strength, for reward. He turns heart and hands and eyes toward his King and Captain. Salvation lies in that direction. Damnation lies in the other.

And all this is not changed because this struggling soldier of God may be again and again beaten down, trampled on, and bruised into the dust. That the soldier is ridden down by overwhelming enemies in the fierce charges of the battle, does not make his foes any less his foes, or himself any less their enemy. Wounded, or captive, he is not their man on that account. He belongs to the other side still.

It is not, by any means, an easy position to hold; and yet it is the very foundation of the Christian life that a man do hold it; that under no circumstance he change his thought about sin, wrong, falsehood; that under no temptation he fail to recognize these as the one curse and ruin to be fought with to the end.

From its first inception to its perfect triumph, repentance, we need scarcely say, is represented in the Gospel as the gift of God. The whole illumination of mind which leads to it—the convincing of sin and of righteousness, and of a coming judgment—is the work of the Holy Spirit. And the strength to hold the conviction to the end, the "light to see his foeman's face," and the power to stand armed and facing him, are the gift of the same Spirit. (2)

That we take all along with us. But we seek here to be clear as to what this foundation is. We want to tell men, seeking repentance under a mistake laid on them, by an emasculated popular religionism, what repentance really is.

The Gospel squares with human nature's needs, and life's necessities. When we clear it of the technical phrases of metaphysic theology, and reduce it to plain English, as it was preached eighteen hundred years ago in plain Greek, we find it commends itself to practical and reasonable men still.

The man who seeks repentance, has but to turn round on his sin, and strike at it with all his power. His sorrow, his internal struggle, his bitterness of grief may be less or more. The point is that he shall know his friends, and know his foes, and in GOD's Name take his place as a redeemed man.

He has but to rise, and looking at the ruin that is dragging him down, face it, as GOD's man, for just what it is, *utter ruin to him ;* and fight it, and, if need be, die fighting it, knowing that to be the only course of salvation for him or any being made, as he is, in GOD's image and not the devil's, in this world or in any world, where the LORD is King.

CHAPTER V.

THE KINGDOM.

FAITH believes the Gospel of Salvation. Repentance turns away from the life past, and looks to a new life in the future. What next? "Men and brethren what shall we *do?*" Then comes the rest of the answer —" Arise and be *baptized?*"

Obedience is the next step.

Now, in examining the New Testament, which contains the Gospel of salvation from sin—its guilt, stain, and penalty—we find a good deal said about "the Kingdom of God" or "the Kingdom of Heaven." There are several parables about it. It is compared with leaven; with a net cast into the sea; with a field, where wheat and tares grew together until the harvest; with a mustard seed, which grew into a great tree. The Gospel, itself, is called "the Gospel of the Kingdom." Its preaching is called the "preaching of the Kingdom of God." After our Lord's Resurrection, during the forty days before His Ascension, we are told He spake to His Apostles "of the things pertaining to the Kingdom of God."

When we turn to the Acts of the Apostles, we find that book to be a history of the organization and spread of a certain Society—the Church. In that story, the parables of our Lord are fulfilled. The Kingdom is organized. Its officers are appointed. Its methods of administration are determined. The net *is* cast into the sea. The leaven *is* rapidly leavening the dead mass of human society. The mustard-seed is sprouting, and already there is the promise of the "great tree."

That is to say, the Kingdom of God is not a metaphor. It is not something merely future. It is actually established here on earth. "Behold," said Christ, "I appoint unto you a Kingdom." The Church of God, which we find at once organized and spreading, in the story of the Acts of the Apostles, is the fulfilment of that prophecy.

That "the Kingdom of God is *within you*," does not contradict the fact that the Church is the Kingdom, for that declaration only presents another side of the same truth. Its principles, laws, and life, *must* be within a man, if he is to continue a living member of the Kingdom. In that it differs, entirely, from the kingdoms of this world.

That is to say, in providing for the salvation from sin of the human race, Christ established, here on earth, a polity, distinct and separate from all the kingdoms of the world. He did not propose to leave men to grope on their way, each alone, in darkness and isolation. For their recovery He organized a Kingdom, whose laws are the laws of Heaven, whose life is the life of Heaven, whose organic Head and King is the Lord God Himself.

He proclaimed, here, the laws which men had lost or forgotten, the eternal laws by which the Universe stands, the unalterable laws of God's own nature. They are the laws by which the angels live, by which the archangels stand. They are the laws, too, by which alone men can live, by which alone any creature, in any world, can stand. Amid the anarchy, blindness, and rampant wrong of this rebel world, he organizes a Kingdom on the basis of those laws—a Kingdom for pardoned rebels, for men saved from sin, for children of GOD returning home to GOD again and accepting His law and service as their salvation.

This is the aspect of the Church of GOD presented us in the New Testament.

It is a polity that is clear. It is an organized, visible community. It has its rulers. They are clearly the Apostles of the LORD, who are already "judging the twelve tribes of Israel." It has its other subordinate officers. Deacons we find first, appointed to assist the supreme officers. Then also we find Presbyters or Bishops, as they were called by both names then, subject to the Apostles, who select them and ordain them, discipline and "rebuke" them.

We find this community legislating, passing decrees in public councils and enforcing them.

We find, too, that men have a definite way of entering this polity. It has its naturalization laws, so to speak. A man who is not a citizen can become so by taking certain steps and making certain pledges. All are welcome to enter—grown men and children—by fulfilling the regular requirements of the laws of naturalization.

The supreme law of this Kingdom is the law revealed by CHRIST—the law of Heaven. Towards GOD, the position is that of a son. Towards men, that of a brother. Citizenship in this Kingdom makes a man a son of GOD, and consequently all are brethren; for this Kingdom is also a Family.

That is to say, the supreme law is Love.

The Head of this Kingdom is CHRIST. The Life of this

Kingdom is the HOLY SPIRIT. He dwells in it forever. He fills all its operations, and gives them all their force. He is in it to help and sustain every member, and to bind him into living, organic unity with the Head.

We take the Church to be, then, an essential of the salvation wrought out for men by CHRIST. This polity, community, kingdom or family, is divine, and necessary to the purposes of the LORD. He contemplated its establishment from the first. He speaks of it throughout all the Gospels. He discourses largely of its nature. He promises its establishment, and, amid all discouragements, its final success. "Art thou a king then?" PILATE asks. "For this cause came I into the world," is the answer. To be King of this Kingdom of GOD, planted as a colony of Heaven, here in this rebellious and ruined earth, our LORD declares to be the cause of His mission.

The understanding of the nature and purpose of the Kingdom of GOD simplifies greatly our comprehension of human duty and the method of individual salvation. It is because, in so much of our modern preaching, no place is found for this Kingdom, which fills so large a space in the New Testament, that so many are confused and misled when they wish to do their duty.

It was organized to take in all who want to accept the freely-offered salvation and to make the common gift their *own*. It was made to be the city of refuge for all souls fleeing from the destruction of a ruined earth. Here GOD's laws and not the world's were proclaimed. Here the Kingship and Sovereignty of the LORD, righteous and true and unchangeable, were announced as eternal facts of *human* life. Here, man's eternal King, Master, and Father was enthroned on earth once more, for the love and obedience of His children. It was a true and veritable Kingdom, a real State and Polity, demanding, as its right, the allegiance of all humanity.

We read of a course of good works "*before* ordained for us to walk in." In the nature of the Kingdom this text finds its fulfilment. The whole course of right living on which a man is to enter, the whole road of obedience on which he is to travel, the works which he is to do to "work out his own salvation," are all arranged beforehand in the Kingdom. He has not to wander off into blind paths to find his life or its works. He is not left to be his own guide over the wastes of the world. His path is marked out. His duty lies at his hand. Here is the Kingdom of GOD with its eternal laws, its unvarying duties, its fixed principles towards GOD and man. Inside it lies his Christian life. It stands here to take him in.

Therefore "the LORD," we read, "added to the Church, daily, *the saved.*" "Such as should be saved," the common version has it. It is literally "*the saved.*"

For, already, having left their rebellion, having forsworn the devil, the world and the flesh, having turned heart and soul to their battle with sin, having entered on the "good works before ordained," *they were saved,* as a literal and present fact, of life and experience.

Within this Kingdom, too, lies the central fact of Christianity as a life; the fact we have already mentioned—the presence of the HOLY SPIRIT.

Here is the broad distinction between CHRIST's religion and all human systems.

He not only lays down the road. He provides help to

travel it. He not only demands righteousness. He also gives grace to follow righteousness.

This Church is, we are told, the dwelling place of the Spirit of God. Through it all runs the divine power of that Spirit. The man, in the Kingdom, has the gifts of Grace. He is in a realm of spiritual life and strength. He is surrounded and sustained, on all hands, and from all the sources of worship, prayer, praise, and sacrament, by the living tides of spiritual power which flow from the Lord and Life-Giver.

For this Kingdom is not only a Kingdom. It is not a *mere* polity. It is more than a mere society. This wondrous Kingdom is a *living organism*—a body—a living, growing, thinking, feeling, working body.

The man inside, is a member of that body. He partakes its force, its blood, its life. He is bound fast, in his place and position, to the whole, and the whole to him. He cannot suffer but a thrill of pain runs through the vast whole. He is sustained by all the power of the great Kingdom. He shares its life. He is victorious in the Omnipotent Spirit that makes him, also, the Temple of God.

So it is "the Kingdom of Grace," and succors the weaknesses of man by the indwelling power of God.

St. Paul, within it, writes—"I can do all things through God, who strengtheneth me."

CHAPTER VI.

OBEDIENCE—BAPTISM.

PRACTICE is the end of all theory ; action the end of all instruction. " What shall we *do?* " is the one only sincere and sensible question when a man hears the Gospel and believes it.

The answer given was double—" Repent and be baptized. " That was the answer at first, and it must be the answer to the end.

We have considered the former part of it. Let us now examine the latter—" be baptized. "

We have seen that our LORD organized, here on earth, a Kingdom. It was to be governed, this Kingdom, by the everlasting laws of heaven. Its subjects were to stand on the same organic law, on which the angels stand and serve in the courts of GOD. To them amnesty was to be given for past rebellion ; free pardon, bought by the SAVIOUR, was to be freely conferred for all past breaches of the law ; and they were enrolled henceforth as subjects and servants of the only Master and King.

That is the way in which that organization—the CHURCH—presents itself in the New Testament. It stands among the Kingdoms of the earth, distinct and solitary ; setting aside their differences ; ignoring distinctions of rank, place, or nationality ; knowing " neither Jew nor Greek, neither bond nor free, " neither Emperor nor beggar ; but ranking them all as one in the one

brotherhood—the great, endless, world-embracing new
"Kingdom of Heaven."

Now, all who believed the Gospel were told to "repent,"
to change their entire aim and purpose and views for life,
and enter this Kingdom, and live on its laws hencefor-
ward.

The method of entrance instituted by the LORD Himself
was *Baptism*.

He adopted a simple and significant rite, with which
the people had been long familiar, as the form of naturalization into this Kingdom. In that rite the King and
His rebel subject meet. They enter, there, into agree-
ment. The rebel renounces his rebellion, forswears
allegiance to all the tyrants that have usurped authority
over him, denies their service, rejects their names, and
takes forever the oath of allegiance to his rightful LORD
and King, and vows to serve Him faithfully his life long.

This, on the man's part. On the King's part there
was the pledge of forgiveness, the promise of acceptance,
the assurance of protection from the hostile tyrants, the
help of the abiding SPIRIT as his ghostly ally in all times
of danger and fear. And the LORD left the administration of this covenant, and the authority to act in His
Name in reconciling men and GOD, to the officers of this
Kingdom for all time—"Go ye into all the world and
make all nations disciples, baptizing them in the name of
the FATHER, and of the SON, and of the HOLY GHOST.
And lo! I am with you always, even to the end of the
world."

Simply and clearly, Baptism was thus the acceptance
of GOD's service, the naturalization into His eternal
Kingdom.

It was the first act of obedience, and symbolized,

expressed, and concentrated all the rest. It was the first *act* to be *done ;* and it meant a whole life of obedience following. The man, a rebel before, stood up before men and angels, before earth and heaven, and renounced the slavery of his rebellion, and took the solemn oath of loyalty to his forgiving King.

He was *saved* in the act. We cannot see how any other word will express the result. He was *lost* in his rebellion. He turns, accepts the amnesty, swears himself into the Kingdom of Mercy and Grace, of Righteousness and Love, and *is saved.*

Understanding what Salvation is—deliverance, not only from the penalty, but from the guilt and stain and power of sin ; and understanding what God's Kingdom is—the ordered polity formed here on earth, under the eternal laws of heaven ; and, also, understanding what Baptism is—the covenant by which man renounces his sin, and enters the Kingdom whose law is Holiness—understanding these things, we can also understand the high things which the Scriptures speak of Baptism and its effects.

For the whole is consistent. The New Testament proclamation of these things goes all together as one clear whole. We need do violence to no statement. We need pass over no Scripture. We need "explain away" no distinct declaration.

It is only because men have made a theory of " Salvation " which is not the Scriptural one, or a theory of "the Church" which is merely human, or a theory of "repentance " or "faith " which is not in the New Testament, that they are compelled, for consistency's sake, to make a theory also of Baptism which requires them to pass over silently, or to do violence openly, to the plain words of the Lord and His Apostles.

It is our comfort to belong to a Church which fears no Scripture; a Church which has no human theory or system to support; and which, therefore, takes her children by the hand, in sure confidence, at all her worship, and bids them listen to the voice of the Lord and His Apostles.

"The like figure whereunto even Baptism doth also now save *us*," saith St. Peter.

If my theory of Salvation be that it means *only* final deliverance from hell, I must explain away the text. For no man ever held that Baptism assures a man of *perseverance to the end*.

But Salvation, being deliverance from the power of sin, its guilt and stain, here, in this world, a man is most surely *saved* the moment he rises and sincerely denies sin, and faces it as his deadly foe in God's Name, and turns and pledges his life to righteousness and truth in the vows of Holy Baptism.

So the Apostle calls it "the laver of regeneration," and "the washing of regeneration."

And here, Apostles and the entire Church Catholic, only follow the Master.

For Nicodemus coming to Him by night, to ask Him of this Kingdom which He, the Prince of Israel, was come to set up, is told by the Lord Himself, "Except a man be born of Water and of the Spirit, he cannot enter into the Kingdom of God."

We cannot pass over the word *Water*. We cannot explain that word away. We cannot suppose the Lord was misleading the anxious enquirer. If our theories of "the Kingdom of God," or of entrance into it, require us to deal unfairly with the words of the Son of God, it is surely time to revise our theories!

It *is* a New Birth. The words fairly express the meaning of Baptism. No other words will do. We cannot spare them in their utter emphasis. Baptism, if we have been clear, *is* Regeneration, a literal New Birth. A man denies his whole past life. He flings away his whole past purposes. He rejects the masters he has served hitherto—the World, the Devil, and the Flesh. He flies to his rightful LORD and King. He knocks for admittance into the New Kingdom founded on earth. He is naturalized into it. He becomes a subject and citizen there. He puts himself under new laws. He is accepted, so flying. GOD receives him coming from his enemies, bruised and wounded. He takes him into the Kingdom of Love and Mercy and Goodness. The man receives the appointed sign and seal of pardon and acceptance. He is literally *new born* into the realm of light and truth, into the Kingdom of Heaven. He is borne out of chaos, darkness, and the anarchy of Satan, into life and light and order, eternal and divine!

We wonder how men stagger at GOD's gracious words. But the wonder goes when we consider how they miss the earnest, downright, practical meaning of CHRIST's religion.

They let it slip away in metaphor. They dissolve it into mere personal feeling. They do not grasp it in its utterly practical proclamation, as a rebinding of rebel subjects, pardoned and accepted by the merits of CHRIST's death and passion, to the service of their LORD. Distinct and pronounced enough, in the New Testament, as a life-long war with SATAN and for CHRIST, in the doing of all good works, they have changed it from a service steadfast, loyal and true, while a man lives, to some mere security against deserved punishment when a man dies. Selfish in all, they have consecrated selfishness by turning it into a religion.

The Church is "the Household of God," saith the Scriptures. The covenant by which a man is adopted into God's Family and becomes His son, (if a man know once what that means to the uttermost,) is surely a New Birth. And God's Household is no metaphor. His Kingdom is no figure of speech. Membership in it is no shadowy dream. Baptism is no empty rite for admission into an obscure sect.

These things are all practical, sensible realities, preached here plainly in a busy, practical world. Christianity is a *life*, and not merely a system of theological opinion.

CHAPTER VII.

The Course of Good Works.

THE doctrine of the Catholic Church about Baptism, if we have succeeded in making ourselves at all understood, is, it will be seen, a part of a great whole. It fits and belongs to her doctrine about Salvation and the rest. To men who do not understand, or who do not accept those doctrines, whether within or without the Church, "Baptismal Regeneration" may, we can readily conceive, seem a shocking doctrine enough. But it is their theories that make it so. The fault is in their systems and not in the doctrine. Their systems, too, (and this is the worst of the matter,) compel them to deal unfairly with, or to explain away, plain declarations of the Word of God.

People brought up in these systems often ask "But do you believe that a man will be saved by being baptized?" The answer is, "We make no prophesies at all. Religion is a present thing. It is not a matter of guess-work. It is a thing which is to be dealt with *now*. We believe a man baptized in repentance and faith *is* saved, as a matter of fact, *to-day*. He is *now* saved, if he has been sincere in his vows and turnings to the Lord. Whether he *will be* saved to-morrow, or next year, or after he dies, depends upon his own truth and faithfulness."

That is, the question and the answer evidently go upon

totally different views of salvation. In the question, *to be saved* means to be pardoned and made secure against any suffering. In the answer, *to be saved* means to be brought into living unity with GOD, and consequently to be delivered from sin.

"Even Baptism doth also *now* save *us*," saith the Apostle. He plainly puts it down as a present matter, a question to be settled just here, this question of salvation.

Now, in explaining here to practical and plain people, certain things in religion, we take into account the fact that systems and theories have put technical and unnatural senses upon plain words, so that when people hear those words in connection with religion, they, unconsciously may be, give them a sense entirely different from what the words would convey, if used about some matter not theological.

And we have desired to bring the mind of the reader back to the fact that when the words were first used, they had no technical sense at all. They were the plain common words of the plain common people, conveying a plain, straight-forward meaning. We shall best understand the Word of GOD by remembering this. It was written and preached long before "the Calvinistic system," or any other "system," except its own plain story of deliverance, was made known to men.

When, therefore, our LORD declares that a man must be "born again of water and the Spirit," it is to be remembered that He does not mean "born again," in the Calvinistic sense, or the Lutheran sense, but in the Gospel sense. And when the Apostle calls Baptism "the washing of regeneration," it is to be carefully considered that he does not mean Calvinistic regeneration, nor

Methodist regeneration, but New Testament regeneration. When, again, we are told that " Baptism doth also *now save us*, " we are to reflect that the Apostle does not say that it saves us in the Wesleyan way, or in the Lutheran way, or in the Roman Catholic way, or in the Sweden- borgian way, but in the Gospel way.

Plain as all this is when one thinks, we need to state it often, because men are continually making the Word of God of none effect, in many ways, by their sect tra- ditions. The sect "system" gives a particular technical meaning to some words in the Scriptures. That technical meaning, if applied to the word in certain connections, will evidently contradict the "system." Therefore, the word is passed over, or explained away, into metaphor or figure. Instead of seeing and confessing that, in this case, the "system" or "theory " is wrong, and rejecting it, men still cling to the "system," and reject the Scriptures.

So it has come to pass with all those strong and clear expressions about Baptism and its effects in the New Testament. Human "systems" of theology, human "plans of salvation, " have made them only confusions and stumbling blocks. They must be got out of the Scriptures for the consistency of "the system. "

" Baptism, " according to the New Testament, " doth now save us." It is the "washing of regeneration." A man is " born again of water and the Holy Ghost. "

We need to explain away nothing here. By Baptism, a man is entered into the family of God, naturalized into the Kingdom of Grace. He has turned away from rebel- lion and sin, and has solemnly vowed his life, himself, to the Lord Jesus Christ, in the prescribed way, and has been accepted. He is now, therefore, a *saved man*. He is delivered from the sinful world—emancipated from the kingdom of Satan—and is an accepted servant of GOD.

He is, of course, pardoned. Forgiveness is at the very door. There can be no service without forgiveness first. A man cannot enter GOD's Kingdom at all without receiving the benefit of the universal amnesty proclaimed from the Cross of Calvary, eighteen hundred years ago. He is not only pardoned, coming in repentance and faith at the door, but he has also entered into the region of pardon for life. Forgiveness is the law of the kingdom into which he has been received—a part of its organic law, too—its constitution. The man lives in the land of pardon. His abiding relation to GOD is that of a pardoned rebel. He has made a covenant—a signed, sealed and delivered contract—with GOD, securing him grace, amnesty and oblivion of all his past rebellion and wrong-doing. "Arise and be baptized and *wash away thy sins*"—so speaks the bold and unfaltering Word of GOD. We need have strong suspicion of our "popular Christianity," when it dare not repeat such a plain statement of inspiration.

Pardoned, then, amnestied, with sins "washed away," and "born again" into the organized Kingdom of GOD, a man is, in the fullest sense, saved; and the Church is to go on, as at the first, receiving "*the saved*," whom GOD adds to her, "day by day."

But this clearly is but the beginning. The man has but taken the first step on the road. He *is* saved, so far. Whether he go on and *stay saved*; whether he will walk the road of salvation to the end; whether he will fight the bitter battle with the world, the flesh, and the devil, through to a victorious issue; whether he will "abide to the end," and be saved at the end, as he is at the begin-

ning, depends upon himself and his use of the grace of
God given him.

His membership in the Kingdom puts him on the
Christian road. The road lies still before him, stretching
on to the gates of paradise. His admission into God's
household lays before Him the whole "course of good
works before ordained, that he should walk in" them.
The good works are all to be done still. His covenant,
sealed in Baptism, binds him over to a life-long service
and obedience. The service is still to be given—the obedience still to be rendered.

Into his position plainly enter yet the elements of
human weakness, vacillation and unfaithfulness. He
has *begun* a good course. That is all.

Therefore, we have, in all the Epistles, written to the
baptized, it must be remembered, to men addressed as
"saints," as "elect," as "justified," as "called," as
"sanctified," warnings often and strong against sin.
In all these Epistles we have the possibility of final
failure taken for granted; indeed, dwelt upon and urged
as a fearfully powerful motive for watchfulness and
faithfulness. Even St. Paul proclaims his discipline of
his body, stern and steady as it was, as induced by the
possibility, that after he had preached the Gospel to
others, himself might be "a cast-away."

Therefore, these men are warned—"called," "elect,"
"saints," as they are named—to "work out" their
"own salvation with fear and trembling."

In plain words, a man has to do the duties of his
position henceforth. He has to fight out the fight to the
end. He has to struggle on, step by step, upon the
upward road. He has to win an inch to-day and another
to-morrow. He has to cleanse his heart of one and

another evil root of sin, day by day. The meaning of his Baptism is, that in it he solemnly, before GOD and man, undertook all this. He is saved in doing it. Just as long as he keeps to the work he remains saved. He was saved the hour he entered on it. He is saved all the day, and every day he works at it. Just so long as a man in GOD's name, and by the power of His grace, fights sin in him and about him, and refuses to do anything with it, except fight it, just so long is he a saved man. It is impossible that a human soul, holding that attitude, should be anything but saved anywhere. Baptism saves, because in it a man takes that attitude, and is placed in the Kingdom of Grace, where he is helped to keep it while life lasts. Whether he shall "continue in that state of salvation until his life's end," is another question.

The Gospel offers him the means to continue—all the helps required for steadfastness. These we are to look at still.

CHAPTER VIII.

CONFESSING CHRIST.

BAPTISM, being a birth, as we have seen, into GOD'S Kingdom, is the beginning of life and work and duty. It is ONLY the beginning. All the questions of life are to be answered yet.

There is nothing about which men are so commonly and so obstinately wrong, as about the matter of confessing CHRIST. They have a notion that a man in that act is professing to "have got religion," as it is sometimes called, or to have "met with a change," as others call it—to have received, that is, some special visitation, some peculiar gift, or grace, or blessing, or call, which cuts him off from common sinners and puts him among the number of "the elect," the "converted" —the special favorites of heaven.

We need not inquire here after the false "system" of "decrees," and "effectual calls," which, although itself long dead, has left this, among other things, as a legacy to "our common Christianity." We find it everywhere, this utterly false and anti-Christian notion, which turns into mockery and nonsense the invitations and warnings of the Scripture and the Church.

A man is invited, warned, pressed, to confess CHRIST; to take His name and service and law upon himself; to come to Him, as a helpless sinner, for help—to Him who never yet turned a deaf ear to any human cry; and all the time the man thinks he is invited, warned, or pressed to profess *himself;* that *he* " has got religion," namely; that *he* "has met with a change"; that *he* has an "experience" to tell; that *he* is a "converted" man.

In truth, among the vast mass whose Christianity is learned from the average common pulpit, we find that it is considered the very purpose and end of "joining the Church," that people may profess themselves different from others; that, not indeed, until they are different—not publicans and sinners at all, but specially gifted Pharisees, and "not as other men are"—are they prepared to "join the Church." For the "Church" is a community of holy people; of people who have been "changed" and "converted"; not of poor struggling sinners, trying to work out their own salvation; and a man has no right to enter it until he is entitled to rank himself among the select circle of the favorites of heaven! Although the whole system on which this notion logically rests is dead and gone, it has left this and other detached fragments of doctrine in the common mind; and a man will find, if he inquire, that the invitations of the Gospel convey no meaning to scores of people in the pews, because confessing CHRIST with them means professing that they "have got religion," and are thus different from other people. They are pressed to come forward and take the vows of the LORD upon them in Baptism, or to renew them in Confirmation; and they imagine all the time, that they are invited to come and profess themselves to be better than other people—the possessors of a special and peculiar gift! Indeed, one will often be shocked to find that men and women who have heard the Gospel all their lives, still

suppose that no man ought to come to Baptism or Con-
firmation who is not prepared to stand and make the
Pharisee's "profession of religion"—"God, I thank
Thee that I am not as other men are"!

Again, there are others, frequently, who want to do
their duty; who wish to rank themselves on the side of
Christ; who desire to enter on the labor of their lives,
as He has taught it; and they are held back for years,
and perhaps for all their lives, because they do not meet
with that experience, or visitation, or call, which, as they
suppose, is their necessary title to His favor.

Now, clearly, there is nothing of all this in the cases
of Baptism related in the New Testament. The qualifications there are repentance and faith. Every man who
believes, and desires to lead a new life, is urged to
"arise and be baptized."

In Baptism a man professes nothing about himself.
He comes as a poor, helpless sinner, with the same
claims upon his Saviour that are possessed by every
beggar—the claims of his own weakness and sinfulness.
He stands before God, as all men must stand, *in forma
pauperis*, in beggar's guise. The claim of every publican
and every magdalen, of every poor penitent sinner over
the whole world, is his claim, the only claim that Christ
can receive—"I am not come to call the righteous, but
sinners, to repentance."

He enters the Kingdom of God, then, not because he
is a good Christian already, and therefore entitled to
come into that select circle, but because he wants to become
a good Christian and lead a true Christian life. He
enters that Kingdom because there are the helps and
graces which he needs; because he finds the air and
food to sustain his spiritual nature. The Church is, in

this view, a school for the moral training of the helpless and the ignorant. Still farther, it is an hospital where sick souls are gathered to be healed. He finds care there, patient watchfulness and thoughtfulness there. He finds light and comfort, and air and medicine there. He asks admittance because he *is* ignorant and helpless, because he *is* deadly sick.

The Church of God is the crown and perfection of the divine arrangement of this world as a school of probation. It completes and makes one the discipline of nature and the family and social life. It is made for imperfect, weak and struggling natures. It is fitted with counsel and comfort and help, with instruction and warning and ever-present aid, that a man may do the work God demands at his hands. It is sad to think how this large, Catholic, and world-enduring work has been lost from the thought of thousands; and that, instead, they have gone on the narrow conception of the Church, as a small religious club, composed of a set of people who have had some special common experience, and have arrived at some special common theory about religion.

We here, are speaking of the Catholic Church of the New Testament, that Kingdom founded by Christ and His Apostles, which claims the allegiance of every soul in the whole world, and to enter which each man's title is the same—the common human nature, and its universal redemption, the universal fall, and the common salvation.

A man is naturalized into that Kingdom by Baptism. He is *born* into it, and begins his life with infancy. Within it are provided all the helps needed to bring that spiritual life to perfection. The Holy Ghost who descended and took possession of the Church as His perpetual dwelling place, upon the day of Pentecost, remains the source and Author of life and power, to all sincere souls within it, till the end of time.

So Christianity, we need to tell men, is a life, and a steady growth. It has its beginning, its progress, its completion. There are "babes in CHRIST." There are strong men in Him. There is food for each class. Milk for the one; strong meat for the other.

There is the steady sound of worship, confession, prayer and praise. There is the ever recurring Sacrament of the Body and Blood of the LORD. There are fasts and festivals, and all the circle of the year which is ruled by the Sun of Righteousness, and which brings in due season to the soul, every fact and doctrine of Christianity. There is the Word of GOD forever preached, in Lesson, in Psalm, in Gospel and Epistle. There is the perpetual setting forth upon the Altar of the Sacrifice of the death of CHRIST. There are warnings in danger, and consolations in trouble. There is thanksgiving for the hour of joy, and sympathy for the hour of sadness. Human life, in all its various experience, is provided for, and all are sanctified, and the soul, in all, looks to and clings to GOD.

And these are called "means of grace"; means, that is, by which spiritual help comes to a man; means by which the strengthening influences of the HOLY SPIRIT are given to the soul. The graces are various, for life is various, and needs are various. The gifts are manifold as are the forms of life in the natural world. But all are from the self-same SPIRIT, who divides unto every man severally as He will.

So the man is placed in the midst of spir l influences; brought into living contact with the eternal and changeless world which lies around him unseen. He is bound fast by eternal bands to GOD, and GOD to him. He grows under the sunlight and dew of heaven. His strength increases daily, as he struggles with the evil he must conquer. His heart is open now to GOD, and stands waiting and spread out for all good gifts from His hand.

Weak himself, incapable, of himself, of doing anything save destroying himself, he looks to be saved, and is saved only by grace through faith, as saith the Apostle. He believes GOD; and, seeking GOD's help in GOD's way—grace where GOD gives it—that grace suffices for him, and in GOD's strength he conquers at last.

CHAPTER IX.

THE RESPONSIBILITY OF CHOICE.

FROM what we have said, it follows that, to profess CHRIST, is in every man's power.

We go farther. To profess CHRIST, is every man's bounden duty.

The pardon is universal. The amnesty is universally offered. Salvation is a free gift to every child of man.

Being so, every man can be saved, if he will.

It comes, therefore, as one of the duties of life in this world, for every man to place himself under the law of CHRIST, to get himself naturalized into the Kingdom of GOD, to take his place as a loyal servant of the KING OF KINGS.

For the two requisites are repentance and faith. They are all we find required by the Apostles, when they first opened the doors of the Kingdom. Every man, with these two qualifications, was not only invited, but commanded to come in.

It must be so to the end. No man can ever demand any terms which are not demanded in the New Testament. The Apostles did not make the Covenant. They only administered it. They did not create its terms. They but announced them. What ST. PAUL, ST. PETER and ST. JOHN could not alter or add to, certainly cannot be improved by Mr. SMITH or Mr. ROBINSON.

There are thousands, we find, who think they have no business to become "professing Christians"—no right to enter the Christian Church. To this hour, in a half dozen different shapes, the old doctrine of restricted salvation, and the "effectual call" rides, like the night-mare, the souls of Americans.

Something must come besides the invitation. The common preaching of the Gospel has no meaning for them. There is to be, above and beyond, some myste-rious visitation, some startling experience, which they can do nothing to bring on, and nothing to delay, which is outside of human resolution and of the course of law and ordinary Providence, which alone gives them the right to become Christians professed. This root lie has wonderful vitality, and is responsible for nine-tenths of the "non-professorism" of America.

There is, however, no waiting about it. The whole responsibility now is in a man's own hands. A plain, straight-forward duty is laid before him. On his own head be it, if he neglect to take it up. Any theory which throws the responsibility of a man's present and eternal damnation upon God, is scarcely Christian, call itself whatever else it may. For a man to wait a life-time, utterly refusing to do a plain duty, utterly denying God in His own world, when he is invited, urged, pressed, commanded, and entreated by the Lord Himself to do it, on the ground that his pleading Saviour does not "convert" him, or "effectually call" him, or send him some mysterious gift over and above the common invitation to all sinners, is so strange a caricature of Christianity, that one could not believe it if he had not seen it.

It is simply the duty of every man to whom the Gospel

comes to accept it. It is his plain next duty to enter the
Church and the Kingdom of God. He has no business
to wait for any call more pressing than the proclamation
of universal salvation. He stands now a rebel. He
acknowledges no allegiance to the King. He is lost every
hour he does so stand. His plain business is to walk
straight away, and ask the first priest who has the right,
to administer to him the oath of allegiance, and to get
the benefits of the amnesty signed and sealed to himself
individually.

The Church of God, as we have seen, is not a voluntary Society. The Kingdom of God is not a club of
man's making. A man is not free to join it or let it
alone, as he is free to join or not to join a Masonic
Lodge or a Debating Society.

It is a Kingdom which a man must enter on peril of
spiritual ruin. Membership in it is a bounden obliga-
tion—God commands it. Christ orders it, with no
exception.

And since the command is universal; since there is no
exception at all in the invitation or the order; and since,
of course, the Lord will have no man enter unprepared,
it follows of necessity that the preparation is in each
man's own hands. Christ's invitations are not a
mockery. He will hold no man responsible for impossi-
bilities. And when He says "come," and when the
Spirit says "come," and when the Bride—the Church
—says "come," and when every one that hears the
Gospel is commanded to say "come," we may be very
sure that the invitation means what it says, and that
every man *can* come who *will* come.

"*But to-day?*" Yes, to-day! For the invitation is
given to-day; the command is to attend to-day; the

proclamation goes over the earth to-day. What sense in this, if invitation and proclamation cannot be obeyed to-day?

It lies, we say, in a man's own hands, this day and every day. It is the one truth that needs to be pressed in, clear, hard, and sharp—blow on blow—upon the consciences of every American congregation, drugged half to death with the fatalism of a dead Calvinism. Men, clear and practical on the limits of their own duty, shouldering like men their own responsibilities in all else, will talk pure Mohammedan fatalism on the question of doing their religious duty, will shirk responsibility then, and blasphemously lay the blame on GOD, that they are living outside His Covenant, rebels and aliens; for are they not waiting till He "converts" them?

The Kingdom of GOD is here, somewhere. If a man does not know where, he can do nothing more essentially necessary than to find out just as soon as possible. But we are writing for people who have made up their minds, more or less decidedly, on that subject. The Kingdom of GOD is here. Outside lies the wicked world. It is here—this Kingdom—to hold "the saved," GOD's adopted children. His pardoned servants, the rebels He has converted at the price of His blood.

And this Kingdom demands every soul's allegiance. It comes with authority and power. It persuades and entreats, but also it commands. It stands night and day with open arms. It holds out the covenant—pardon, adoption, help for all the future, on the part of GOD— repentance, faith, pledged obedience on the part of man. The officers commissioned to execute the contract in the name and stead of the LORD, are here. They stand by Font, and Chancel rail, and Altar. They invite, they warn, they call by all motives.

What is it all for ? That a man may rise up and deny the devil, deny the world, deny his own flesh, deny sin and evil, turn to wrestle with his ruin, and do battle with his spiritual destruction, and so save himself by entering this Kingdom of GOD, and taking the LORD CHRIST for his Master, Lord and Captain, henceforth.

It is a practical world ; and, therefore, a religion from GOD, who rules it, will be practical too. Christianity is so—a downright practical· thing. Its acceptance is a visible fact ; its profession is a plain reality. The change from evil to good is a clear thing, which a man cannot doubt; a plain thing, which he cannot but see. The purpose is to get him, just as soon as possible, at the business of *fighting sin*, which is the great business in this world at least; to make his way just as clear and easy as possible to that Divine warfare. It *is* so made. Five minutes is enough for a man who is in earnest, and fifteen will complete his enlistment, and put him under CHRIST's command to fight the devil till he dies. It is a short matter, for life is short; and there is an immense amount to be done in it. We cannot spend much in preliminaries. "ARISE AND BE BAPTIZED," is still, as of old, the command. And now, to half the bewildered and sleeping occupants of our pews, the one command of life, and deliverance !

.